FACE TO FACE

FACE TO FACE

CHRISTOPHER ELLIS

Matador
9 De Montfort Mews
Leicester LE1 7FW, UK
Tel: (+44) 116 255 9311 / 9312
Email: books@troubador.co.uk
Web: www.troubador.co.uk/matador

Cover design © Christopher Ellis

ISBN 978-1848760-127

A Cataloguing-in-Publication (CIP) catalogue record for this book is available from
the British Library.

Typeset in 13pt Stempel Garamond by Troubador Publishing Ltd, Leicester, UK

Matador is an imprint of Troubador Publishing Ltd

David was happy. He was on his way to Poole for a day's sailing with some good friends on their boat. The sun was shining, the road was clear and he was listening to a favourite CD. It wasn't often that he found himself on the road this early and he was making the best of the light traffic. A good driver, he was pushing the little car to its limit.

The road curved to the left and he accelerated into the bend, feeling the car drift very slightly on the damp surface. As he corrected, he suddenly saw a deer jump out into the road in front of him. He braked, the car swerved and skidded, he struggled with the wheel but was unable to keep the car on the road. In horror he saw that he was heading straight for a large tree on the verge. He let go of the wheel and covered his face with his arms. There was an enormous crash and he remembered nothing more.

✳

David brought the car to a gentle halt. The figure waving him down seemed familiar. He got out and started walking towards him. Could it be?

"Uncle Andy?" he called.

He began to run and then stopped in amazement.

"Uncle Andy?" he repeated.

"The same," came the reply.

David ran the last few yards towards his uncle and threw his arms round him.

"What on earth are you doing here?" he cried.

"I came to meet you," said Andy.

"But you're…"

"Yes."

"I don't understand," stammered David.

Andy put his arm round David's shoulder and began to walk towards a car that was standing nearby.

"Is this a dream?" asked David hesitantly.

"No, it's no dream," replied Andy. "Come with me and I'll explain."

David stopped suddenly.

"But if you're..." He hesitated. "Then ...?"

"Yes," said Andy.

"But I'm alive," cried David. He glanced down at himself. "And unhurt. What happened?"

Andy stayed silent.

David paused and looked around.

"Where are we?" he whispered.

"We call it heaven," said Andy.

*

Neither of them spoke as Andy drove the short distance to his house. David's mind was in a whirl. He couldn't quite bring himself to believe what deep within him he knew to be true. Feelings of confusion and sadness conflicted with a profound underlying sensation of peace. And everything seemed so natural, so much like the world he had left. Andy's car, for example, a snazzy two-seater, the country around, the few people he saw in the streets during the short drive.

Andy drew up in front of a pretty stone-built cottage on the edge of a small village. He led the way inside and through into a comfortable sitting-room.

"Stay here," he said, disappearing through another door, "I shan't be a second."

David looked around him. The first thing he noticed was the photographs. Every surface was covered with them and they were nearly all familiar to him, mostly of the family but also of Andy's army friends and a few others David didn't recognise. The room was bright and comfortably furnished with a large flat-screen TV taking pride of place by the fireplace. David went up to a mirror hanging on the wall and looked at his face intently. As far as he could tell, he was looking as he always did – entirely normal. He sighed and turned away just as Andy reappeared with two pint mugs of beer. Giving one to David, he said, "You'd better sit down and I'll try to explain a few things."

David sat in an armchair and took a large gulp from his drink. In spite of their previous short conversation, he was now sure he was dreaming. But was it possible to be aware you were in a dream? He didn't know.

"It's a shock when you first arrive, isn't it," said Andy gently, "especially when it's all so sudden. That's why I'm here."

"How did you know?" asked David. "That I was coming, I mean."

"I just knew," said Andy.

There was a pause. David didn't know what to ask first, thoughts whirling through his mind in hopeless confusion. And Andy didn't seem to know where to begin.

"You'll miss Ruth to begin with," Andy said at last, "but then it'll get easier."

David felt a sudden sharp pang of grief.

"Can I see her?" he asked hesitantly.

"Yes, you can," Andy replied, "but you can't talk to her or touch her. It's very very hard because you'll see her grief and not be able to do anything about it. I remember it well."

He smiled.

"But grief here is but a shadow of what it is on earth. You'll be happy, happier than you can imagine, and even when you're sad you'll feel a deep sense of peace." He paused. "It's hard to explain."

David could already feel the sharp pain ebbing away.

"How do I … go back?" he asked hesitantly.

"You just will it," said Andy, "and it'll happen, like everything else here. You can be with anyone you like – as long as they're here too!"

"Grandpa?"

"Yes, you'll see him very soon."

David's mind began to clear. He looked around again at the comfortable room.

"But how do you live?" he asked.

"It just happens," said Andy. "You can eat and drink if you want but you don't have to. The same with sleeping and everything else to do with your body. You can be in any kind of environment you like – and a lot besides, places and scenery like you've never seen on earth."

"And I can do whatever I like?" asked David, eyes widening.

"Whatever you like," replied Andy with a smile.

"Provided it doesn't hurt anyone else."

Andy shrugged. "You'll never do that here," he said simply.

"Sailing?" asked David with excitement.

"Of course. I'll take you out myself one day."

David was silent.

"And what about God?" he asked at last. "Do we meet Him?"

"Of course," said Andy gently.

"But are there ….churches and things?"

"Not as such. God is everywhere. You don't need a building here."

David thought of his own religious life. It hadn't been something of which he could be terribly proud.

"I used to enjoy going to church," he said finally, "and then I stopped, like most other people, I suppose – except for social occasions, weddings, funerals, christenings – and Christmas. But I think I might have gone back to it."

"I was the same," said Andy. "Except we used to have church parades and other occasional services in the Army. I always believed in God, I just wasn't very active. But God knows what's in our hearts, He knows the pressures of life and He never gives up on people. And church isn't everything, important though it is. It's how you lived your life that really matters."

David was struggling to put his thoughts into words.

"But does everyone come here then?" he asked.

Andy paused.

"Not everyone," he said. "There are other places. I don't know more about it than that. There's no contact. I knew someone in the Army once. He was a bit wild and always getting into trouble. He was kicked out in the end and finished up in prison for manslaughter. He died there in suspicious circumstances. I've tried a couple of times to see him but without success. The funny thing is I rather liked him."

"And what about the really good people?" David asked.

Andy smiled.

"They're here," he said. "You can met them. Some will come and see you. You may not know who they are but they'll talk to you and help you understand."

"Who have you seen?" asked David eagerly.

"No-one I'd ever heard of," Andy replied laughing, "but I love talking to them." He paused. "I always thought I was a goodish sort of chap," he went on, "but I wasn't even close!"

"In what way?" David queried.

"In every way. It's almost like things here are a sort of mirror image of how they are on earth. Everything's upside down and back-to-front. As if our human natures made it as difficult as possible to lead a good life. Everything was stacked against it. But here you can see everything so clearly. And it all comes together and makes sense."

"But can we not explain that to people?" asked David. "I mean people back there?"

"No, I'm afraid not," said Andy quietly. "I only wish we could. It seems people have got to try and work it out for themselves. Many people do – a surprising number – but they don't seem to be able to influence the majority." His face clouded over. "It leads to such huge sadness there. And suffering."

✻

"What do people do here?" asked David.

"As I said before, you can do anything you like," replied Andy. "But 'doing' isn't really what it's all about here. 'Doing' is an earthly thing; it goes with living on earth where you can't survive unless you 'do' something. Here it's more 'being'. 'Human being' is a bad description; it should be 'human doing'! Just think how busy we all were!"

"We had to be," said David a little defensively.

"Of course. But the happiest people were the ones who managed to balance their lives between doing and being. Buddhist monks, for example. Their meditation balanced them and enabled them to live in the world and still find peace – deep inner peace."

"I never did any meditation," said David sadly. "I often thought about it but there was never time."

Andy laughed.

"My point exactly," he said. "I know, I was the same. But don't worry, here you don't need it. As you'll find, it's the natural state to be in. You'll have to make an effort to do anything!"

"The only thing I feel passionate about doing is sailing," said David.

"Yes, people follow their passions here. They're the only things that are done. Which is wonderful. You'll see some of the amazing things people get up to."

There was silence between them. David was tying to absorb what Andy had told him. He was beginning to feel indefinably different.

Until now his thoughts and feelings had almost been human still. Apart from the inner contentment, he felt very much as he had on earth. But now he felt himself changing in a subtle and gradual way. He was almost entirely unaware of his body, as if it wasn't there. He could become aware of it or any part of it if he wanted to but then it slipped back into the background. It suddenly struck him that his body was now his unconscious. So what was his conscious then? His thinking processes seemed unchanged but his feelings of peace, of contentment, of nothing mattering were now his main consciousness. In an extraordinary way he felt turned inside out. The things that had mattered to him on earth were now insignificant. What filled him and consumed him was something he had never known or felt before. Some words of Jesus suddenly came to him.

"He who loses his life shall find it," he murmured.

Andy smiled.

"You're coming along," he said. "Come with me, I want to show you something."

He took David's hand and before David knew what was happening he found himself absorbed and engulfed in the brightest light he had ever experienced. He and Andy were in the middle of a huge mass of people that shifted and moved like a cloud. Sometimes they were pressed on every side; sometimes they were quite alone. But always the white and gold light bathed them in its bright but soft translucence and music of breathtaking beauty swirled around them. Some of it was familiar but much of it was new – strange and mysterious, flowing inexorably on through magical harmonies and rhythms, great climaxes involving what seemed like thousands of voices and periods of almost complete stillness. The music and the light pierced into his very depths and he felt his heart bursting with a joy the like of which he had never even imagined. It was not a passing joy of thrill or excitement but a deep and absorbing happiness which filled his whole being until he himself was an integral part of the light and the sound and the swirling throng. This, he knew, was where he belonged, what he was made for and where he would now for ever be.

＊

David became aware of Andy bending over him. He was back in the armchair in Andy's living-room, the light and the music gradually fading away but never totally disappearing.

"What was that?" he whispered.

"That was God," said Andy. "You felt His presence and His love. You're now a part of Him, as we all are, and He'll never let you go."

"The peace that passes all understanding," David murmured.

"All human understanding, yes," said Andy. "But you'll come to understand it and be a part of it."

"But what have I done...?" began David.

"...to deserve it?" Andy finished for him. "I know. I felt the same. I wasn't a particularly religious person although I always believed in God. But you – and I –

were His children, His creation whom He loved, unconditionally and totally as only He can, in spite of what we were and what we did. You were a decent man and, consciously or not, you lived as best you could. You weren't perfect – neither was I – no-one is on earth. But He never lost faith in you, never abandoned you and always forgave you. And now you're here with Him for ever."

"Can I ... can I see Him?" David asked.

"You have seen Him, and heard Him, and felt Him and now you're a part of Him. You don't have to grapple any more with questions of religion and faith. You'll be given all the answers."

"Now through a glass darkly but then face to face?"

"Exactly."

*

One day he found himself walking through a beech wood. The trees were resplendent with the red and yellow colours of autumn. The sun dappled the soft ground and the leaves of the trees gleamed in the luminous air. It was warm but a light breeze rustled the branches. Beside him walked an elderly woman. She was slight but upright, her hair grey and wiry, her face pale and kindly, a twinkle in her bright blue eyes.

David didn't think they had ever met before but he felt happy in her company. He didn't feel the need to talk nor any discomfort with the silence between them. After a while they came to a glade in the wood from which a broad grassy path ran down to a little stream.

"I love this place," she said as they stopped and looked around. "It's just like a place I used to go to when I needed a bit of peace and quiet."

David wanted to question her about her life but didn't know how to start.

"I needed those moments," she went on. "My husband was a hard man and made life very difficult for us – the children and me. So we used to get away if we could. I had no family to go to and we knew very few people so we used to drive out into the country and let nature do its work." She paused. "I don't blame him," she said reflectively after a moment. "He had a very hard upbringing and took it out on those closest to him."

"Why didn't you leave him?" David asked.

"I did in the end," she said. "I thought he was going to kill me – he was very violent – and I managed to escape with the children to a friend's house. The next day he ran over a mother and child on a pedestrian crossing and killed them. His excuse was that he didn't know what he was doing, he was so devastated by our running away. But he was convicted and sent to prison for two years. He had a record of violence."

"Did you see him again?"

"Oh yes, I took the children to visit him every week. After all, they were his children and he loved them. It took him a long time to accept me but he did in the end and at least he stayed in touch with the children."

"Did you forgive him?" David asked.

"Yes," she said simply. "Yes, I did. I never hated him. In fact I felt sorry for him. When he came out he came back to us but soon afterwards he got ill and eventually died. I nursed him at home and we made our peace, I'm happy to say."

She was silent for a few moments. A pair of squirrels ran across the clearing and leaped up the trunk of one of the trees. David followed them with his eyes as they frolicked in the branches, eventually jumping into another tree and disappearing.

"After he died," she continued, "some friends and I opened a small shelter for people who couldn't stay with their partners.

We heard some terrible stories but I hope we managed to bring some peace into their lives."

"I'm sure you did," said David.

He had never come across domestic violence during his life though he had frequently read about it in the papers. And here was this fragile-looking woman who had not only suffered horrendously herself but had continued to love her persecutor and had devoted her life to helping others who had suffered similar cruelties.

She turned to face him.

"I know what you're thinking," she said, "but don't. I did what I did because that was the sort of person I was. Yes, I suffered, but not more than millions of others. I just did what I thought best."

"I don't think I could have done it," said David.

"You didn't have to," she replied gently. "Everyone has their own unique experience and deals with it as they are able. What is quite easy for one person may be impossible for another. That's why it was so wrong to judge people. Only God can judge."

✳

David never forgot Ruth. She was constantly in the back of his mind. He didn't grieve for himself. He missed her but he knew they would eventually be together again and their happiness would be unbounded. His faith in this was so strong it was almost as if she were already there. But he was sad for her. He knew she would be missing him horribly.

When his thoughts of her were particularly strong, he willed himself to see her. But he never stayed long. He didn't know whether or not she could feel his presence but several times he found her talking to him, sometimes contentedly, sometimes in great distress, sometimes in anger. He felt deeply uncomfortable and totally helpless. All he could do, without knowing whether it would have any effect or not, was to will her his love. Which he did – all the time.

*

"That's amazing, Grandpa."

David was standing in the half-finished kitchen of his grandfather's house. Grandpa had always been a DIY enthusiast and was building this house from scratch, something he had always wanted to do. The structure was complete and he was now working on fitting out the inside, specifically at this time the plumbing. David was astonished at what he had achieved and had forcibly to remind himself that this was a rejuvenated, re-energised Grandpa without any earthly distractions or impediments, in particular no budgetary constraints except those he had voluntarily imposed on himself; he wouldn't be happy if it were too easy.

"Well, I just hope your grandmother likes it when she gets here," said Grandpa a bit gloomily.

David smiled to himself knowing very well that there was nothing his grandfather would enjoy more than changing things, even to the extent of a complete rebuild.

"I just hope it's ready for her," he said putting concern into his voice.

"Oh, it will be," said Grandpa confidently. "Anyway she's quite used to living on a building site," he added dismissively. "Now, come and have a look outside."

He led the way out of the front door onto a levelled patio area surrounded by grass. Some flowerbeds had been cut out but were so far empty of plants. The lawn sloped down and away from the house and merged into an area of parkland dotted with trees. Beyond the park was a valley, green and fertile, which curved away into the far distance. The view was breathtaking.

"What a wonderful spot," exclaimed David.

"Isn't it," said Grandpa. "It took me a while to find, mind you, and it's not perfect, but I think it'll do."

David grinned, remembering how long it had taken his grandparents to choose the site of their last house and the frustration his grandmother had felt, and often expressed, when a site that seemed ideal to her was rejected for some spurious reason that she found incomprehensible. It was a wonder that Grandpa had even got this far.

"Come round to the back and we'll have a cup of tea."

They walked round the house and Grandpa led the way into a small mobile home standing in what would evidently be an enclosed yard.

"This is home for the moment," he said.

While he was making the tea, David took the opportunity to study him. He had last seen him just before he died – old, worn out and in pain. Yet here he was, leaping around, apparently fit as a fiddle, back to the active energetic man David loved to remember and had so much admired. Only his face showed any sign of ageing but this was reduced to insignificance by the bright lively gleam in his eyes.

"You look well, Grandpa," he said, immediately realising what a foolish remark it was.

"Of course I'm well," came the brusque retort; "no problems here. It's wonderful to be able to do all the things I want. This is my third attempt, you know. The first two didn't really work out so I abandoned them and started again."

David had no difficulty believing this. In fact he would have been surprised if it had been otherwise.

"Have you had much help?" he asked.

"Not much," Grandpa answered, "just for the really heavy stuff. Andy's been over a few times. I expect he told you."

"Not yet," said David, "but I'm sure he will."

He looked around the small snug interior and noticed among the photographs a few of handsome-looking cattle and sheep sporting brightly coloured rosettes.

"Have you got any livestock?" he asked, remembering his grandfather's enthusiasm for the animals on their farms.

"Only for decoration," replied Grandpa. "Did you notice the deer in the park? Five different varieties. But there's no need for farming cattle or sheep here." He looked up at the photographs. "You know," he said, "not having to rear livestock for food makes you see the whole business quite differently. It was terrible the way we treated animals and poultry. All that factory-farming and mass production. I'm glad I saw the light and started that protest movement. It didn't achieve a huge amount but it made a bit of a splash locally and made people think." A smile lit up his face. "Do you remember when we let out all those chickens?" He chuckled. "A bit irresponsible really but it made the point and we got a lot of publicity."

David remembered it well. He had been both deeply shocked and hugely proud of his grandfather's behaviour.

"I don't think Granny approved," he said laughing.

Grandpa chuckled again.

"She came round. I seem to remember

she found more eggs than any of us over the next few days!" His face became serious again. "But it was horrible the way animals were treated. Reduced me to tears sometimes. I know you've got to eat – they were put there for us – but it's got to be done humanely."

He was silent, gazing across the yard to the half-finished house.

"Did you know I was put up for an honour?" he asked.

"No," said David. "What happened?"

"Well, it was all that stuff we were doing with farmers, the countryside and so on. Some friends got together and sent my name in. It was going through apparently but when I ended up in court they dropped it like a hot potato!" He burst out laughing. "Didn't want the wretched thing anyway. Stupid system!"

David laughed too at his grandfather's cheery dismissal of something most people would have given their eye-teeth for. He realised how little he had really known him, not surprising as they'd hardly ever seen each other, but he looked forward to spending time with him now.

✳

David and Andy were sitting overlooking a stretch of calm blue water. A few boats were still out there in spite of the lateness of the hour. The wind had dropped and the setting sun lit up the sky with a soft pink glow and touched the rims of the high clouds with gold.

They had been sailing together and David was feeling happier and more at peace than he could ever have believed possible. Andy had taught him to sail as a boy and awakened in him an undying passion. It had been wonderful to have been out there with him again doing what they both loved.

They had talked of many different things during their day together and David really felt he was beginning, just beginning, to understand the nature of his new life. Many questions still remained but they weren't bursting to get out as they had been on his arrival. All except one, involving Andy personally, and he had been waiting for the right moment to put it to him.

Silence fell between them. The sun had set completely now and the sky was beginning to darken. Some lights appeared across the water and were reflected in its mirror surface. David thought carefully how best to broach the subject in his mind.

"I know what you're thinking," said Andy softly.

David looked at him.

"You want to know what I think about my life as a soldier and how it's compatible with life here?"

David stared out over the darkening water.

"Yes, I did want to ask you about that," he admitted, "but I didn't know how best to put it."

"It's a good question," sighed Andy, "and I've given it a lot of thought." He leaned forward in his seat. "I was beginning to have doubts about it even before…" he hesitated, "…before I arrived here courtesy of a Taleban bullet. Doing what we were doing didn't make any sense, far from home, trying to protect people who didn't trust us, against an enemy that was never going to give up." He paused. "It's not the politics of it though," he went on slowly. "Even if the cause had been a good one, I would still have had the doubts."

He paused again and when he continued his voice was so soft that David had to strain to hear him.

"Now I have no doubts. It is all so clear, so horrifyingly clear. Jesus said: 'Thou shalt not kill' but we didn't think it applied to us, we thought it was for civilians. How could it apply to us when we were fighting for a good cause, so we were told, against people who would kill us if they got the chance?"

Andy's voice was getting stronger and his words coming faster. David could only sit motionless and stare out into the darkness.

"I killed then," Andy went on, "and I killed in Iraq and I killed in the Falklands.

That's what we were trained to do – to kill. That was the whole purpose of our existence as soldiers – to kill the enemy before he killed you. I've never forgotten the first one, an Argentinian soldier. I was considered a fine shot and was placed in a good position waiting for them to appear. I got the first one with one shot. He went down like a felled tree. And I rejoiced! I actually rejoiced! Afterwards I had awful doubts. Was it right? Was it justified? For a piece of real estate in the middle of nowhere? He had a mother and father, brothers and sisters, perhaps a wife, perhaps even children. And I took away his life. I was the cause of their grief."

He paused, then went on, "But then it happened again and didn't seem so bad that time. And then again, and again. And we watched bombs raining down and cheered. In Iraq and Afghanistan we killed civilians - men, women and children. We didn't cheer that of course but we didn't worry about it particularly either. It just happened. It was an accident. 'Collateral damage', as the Americans called it."

He was silent for what seemed like an age as David waited for him to continue.

"Towards the end," he went on at last, "all the doubts came back and I was getting near the stage of asking for compassionate leave. Maybe I got careless, perhaps subconsciously wanting to be wounded so I'd be invalided home. I don't know. But I used to pray to be forgiven for what I and the others were doing."

He turned and looked at David.

"I know now that God answered that prayer. I know that He forgives me. And I know now that war is evil, all war, whatever it's about, however just it may be made to appear – and the Church didn't help in that respect with their theories of a 'just war' – because killing is wrong. We are appealed to on the grounds of patriotism and nationalism but there is no justification for taking another human being's life, not even the execution of murderers. Each and every human life is precious to God."

He paused.

"And think about the awful damage

done by nations to their young men and women. Not only are they thrown into mortal danger but they are scarred for life. Some of them can never lead normal lives again. And for what? National pride! Patriotism! What a terrible waste! What terrible suffering is caused!"

He was silent again, his expression bleak.

"I remember listening to a debate about war once," he went on, "and some general got up and asked the pacifist speaker what he would have done against the Nazis. Would he have let them invade, set up concentration camps, continue their murderous policies? "Yes," replied the pacifist simply, "and if necessary I would have died because I know that death is not the end but only the beginning." Wonderful words and I never forgot them even though I pooh-poohed them at the time. And now here we are and we know those words are true."

He paused and turned away. David could hear the distinctive cry of the curlews on the water's edge. The moon had risen and was bathing the water and the shoreline where they were sitting with a mysterious silvery glow. Stars twinkled in the clear black sky.

"There's such fear of death on earth, isn't there," Andy went on quietly. "Of course it can be very unpleasant and grief is a horrible horrible thing to have to suffer. But death itself is nothing to be afraid of and life after death is... well, here we are!" he finished turning to David. "You know."

"Yes, I know – now," said David, "but I didn't then and to me death was pretty much the end of everything. We didn't think about it much at our age. Not like you who were forced to confront it every day of your life. It must have been awful, feeling as you did."

"It was."

Andy was silent for a moment and then went on, "I did consider ending my life once or twice – an insane act of bravado or a simple bullet to the brain. But that's not the answer. It's very understandable sometimes, people find themselves in terrible predicaments, but it's wrong. God put each one of us on earth for a reason. Very often we didn't understand what that reason was but we had a duty to live our lives through to their natural – or unnatural – conclusion. There was a purpose in our soldiering on even if we never knew or understood it. No, suicide's not the answer. It's playing God, I'm afraid, and none of us is in a position to do that."

He straightened up and stretched, then laughed a little self-consciously.

"End of sermon!" he said.

David smiled.

"I only wish you could preach it to everyone back there," he sighed.

"I don't know if they'd listen," said Andy. "After all, they didn't listen to Jesus. And they're far too busy laying up treasure. As was I," he added hastily, "and you, no doubt."

"Guilty, I'm afraid."

"Funny that," mused Andy, "the importance of money and possessions and what a huge burden it was. And there was never enough, however rich you were. And we went on and on trying to get more and more. It's difficult to understand now, in this place. It means absolutely nothing here."

"Could it have been different, do you think?"

"I don't know," replied Andy slowly. "I really don't know."

*

Out for a stroll one morning, David suddenly felt a small hand in his own. Looking down he saw a little girl walking along beside him.

"What's your name?" she asked.

"David. What's yours?"

"Charlie," she said, starting to skip. "Mum said I should have been a boy."

"Is your Mum here?"

"No," she replied simply. "But everyone's my Mum and Dad."

"Don't you miss them?"

"Of course I do, silly," she said cheerfully. "But they'll be here soon."

"How do you know that?"

"Oh, they're getting on a bit," Charlie replied airily. "Do you like holding hands?" she asked, suddenly changing the subject.

"Yes, I do."

"You should do it more often," she said, looking up at him. "Anyway, 'bye."

As she skipped off, David still felt the warmth of her little hand in his.

Yes, he told himself, I should!

*

"Their values are all topsy-turvy." His powerful voice filled the room. "They value strength, force, ruthlessness, power; no consideration is given to the meek or the weak – they're just swept aside. They value wealth, not just as a means to power but as an end in itself; poverty is the greatest misfortune - the poor are of no consequence. They value celebrity, good looks, sexiness, all that is superficial; the plain, the ordinary, the good but humble heart is despised. You have to shout, to repeat yourself over and over, to capture the headlines; there is no place for reason, for modesty, for quiet efficiency. We were all subject to it – even me," he exclaimed, striking his chest as if in penance. "Yes, I was caught up in it just like everyone else – and hated myself for it. I tried hard to resist.

But how do you get your message across in that sort of culture without playing their game? When you've got people's attention, that's fine. But how to get it?"

David had recognised him instantly and now thought back on what he knew of the Reverend Paul Croucher, a firebrand priest who had kicked over the traces of normal priestly life and made a huge name for himself as a Church of England rebel. His message had been that the Church was too rich, too powerful, too concerned with the world and too little involved in the work of ministry. He had been a strong advocate of disestablishing the Church, dismantling its hierarchical structure and disposing of all its wealth and investments, calling instead for a return to the roots of the early Church – local, vigorous, inspired. His final act of rebellion as a serving priest had been to make a bonfire of all the robes, vestments and decorations in his church, having first auctioned off all the silver and valuables and given the proceeds to a charity for the homeless. His congregation were lucky still to have a church – he had tried to set that alight too.

Banished from the Church he had spent the remainder of his life as a wandering preacher, at first talking to anyone who would listen, on street corners or in pubs or village halls. As his notoriety increased, he pulled huge crowds and filled theatres, concert halls and sports grounds. People flocked to hear his simple message of love and forgiveness, the love and forgiveness of God and the love and forgiveness they should show to each other. To the end he remained poor and totally dependant on others' generosity. He forbade anyone to follow him, although many wanted to, and was impervious to material comforts. Finally he died at a grand old age and thousands attended his funeral.

He had come to visit David in his tiny flat – he said he was just passing – and had hardly drawn breath since arriving. David was fascinated. He had never seen him in action – he had died when David was quite young – but had heard much about him. He couldn't take his eyes off him as he strode vigorously up and down the small living-room, occasionally pausing to stare out of the full-length windows that opened onto a balcony overlooking the harbour. He was a tall upright man, his strong weathered face surmounted by a mane of white hair. Sharp eyes shone from beneath bushy white eyebrows. His manner of speaking was declamatory rather than conversational, his words hypnotic.

"It was all topsy-turvy," he was saying again with new energy. "I saw it then. I told them – the Lord knows I told them – loudly and repeatedly." He turned and smiled at David, his face lighting up like a boy's. "No doubt you heard tell of it?"

"Indeed I did. You had the reputation of being the best orator of the century, even better than Winston Churchill!"

"Oh, I don't know," he said, looking pleased. Then his expression turned serious. "But they weren't my words, they were God's. God wanted people to understand, to see, to believe. A simple faith was all that was needed, no learning, no great intellectual powers, just a heart and a mind open to

God's love. Jesus chose his disciples for their simplicity, you know, and called them his children. And he thanked God for revealing himself to simple folk. Those were the people I was speaking to, those the ones who responded."

"You certainly made a huge impact," murmured David. "And your books are still widely read."

"Really?" He swung round and stared at David, then turned away. "But not enough, not enough," he said. "They tried to shut me up, you know, the powers that be – Canterbury, York. But they gave up after a while. They couldn't have stopped me."

He paused and sat down opposite David.

"Where was I? Yes, topsy-turvy - the divine paradox. Fascinating. 'He who loses his life shall save it.' 'The meek shall inherit the earth.' 'Blessed are the poor in heart.' 'By your poverty you will become rich.' It's even in the Old Testament – 'The bows of the mighty are broken and they that stumble are girded with strength.' And so on and so on."

With each quotation he thumped his fist into his palm. His eyes were fixed on David's and David saw in them the strength of faith and commitment that had fired him and kept him going through the long hard years of his life.

"'Why?' people kept asking me. 'Why is it like this?' 'Why is it so difficult?' 'Sell all that you have and follow me.' 'Love your enemy.'"

He paused and gathered his thoughts.

"It's all about death – death, the final frontier. Except that it isn't final and it's a frontier with no immigration, no customs, just a line dividing darkness from light. If you believe death is the end then you'll do anything to avoid it. The survival instinct clicks in and that means, above all, fear. Fear is the great curse of humankind – fear of death, fear of suffering, fear of loss, fear of humiliation. It is this fear that leads to all the evils in the world – violence, cruelty, greed, pride and all the others. Original sin, so much debated and argued over, is simply sin arising from the origins of human life, through evolution back to the animal world. Basic animal instincts are so strong that even God's presence on earth as a human being failed to overcome them. His message was clear. Death is not important. Much more important – vitally important – is doing God's will, overriding the default instincts programmed into us by our origins and looking forward to the wonderful life after death in God's kingdom. Jesus defeated death and assured us this was possible for everybody. That is the good news. That's what he came to tell us."

David felt a growing sense of excitement as he listened – simple words but with such profound meaning. His feelings must have shown on his face for the preacher smiled and leaned forward to touch his hand.

"God gives people a clear choice," he went on, "an unambiguous choice, a choice between two diametrically different ways, not just a fork in the road. You can't be a lukewarm Christian, I used to tell them. You can't be semi-detached. God looks for total commitment, total submission, a total letting-go of earthly values. There is no halfway house. It's no good just taking away half the message – and the easy half at that. It only makes sense in the context of the whole. 'He who is not with me is against me,' Jesus said. Because it's only when you make that total commitment of yourself to God that you can find freedom, perfect freedom. The chains of sin – of pride, of vanity, of self-centredness – fall away and you find peace, the peace that only God can bring, the peace we feel here in His kingdom."

He took David's hand in his and smiled again, that easy boyish smile that warmed your heart. His eyes stared into David's.

"It's yours," he said softly, "yours for ever and ever."

As David looked at him, he felt again that flooding surge of happiness. The golden light of the sun streamed into the little room and played around the tall imposing figure of the preacher. In a brief instant that lasted for ever David saw and understood.

*

He heard the music before he saw the church, one he hadn't noticed before. The open door drew him like a magnet and he tiptoed inside. The interior was spacious and ornately decorated and embellished. He sat down on a chair near the back and closed his eyes. The music surrounded him and filled his being. Intricately complicated, it was yet pure and beautifully simple. Lines of melody emerged, developed and sank back into the rich harmonic texture. The volume rose and fell like waves on the seashore. The notes formed patterns of rich complexity but at the same time spoke directly to his heart.

As he listened, David felt again the white and gold light that had absorbed him on his first encounter with God. It blended with the music and filled his senses so that nothing existed outside this deep and immersing experience. He felt tears well in his eyes and begin to roll down his cheeks.

How long the music continued he couldn't say but at length it came to an end in a falling whispering cadence and silence filled the unlit church. He opened his eyes and saw someone moving slowly past him towards the door.

"Please," he asked quietly, "who was that playing?"

"It was Johann Sebastian Bach," came the answer as the figure glided away.

David remained there a long time, afraid to move and break the spell. Beautiful music had always moved him deeply but he had always fought back the tears and struggled to contain the emotion. Here he felt no such inhibition. With a pang of regret that passed as soon as it struck him, he realised how much richer his earthly experience might have been.

*

"A cup of tea, David dear?"

"Yes, please, Aunt Doris."

"Indian or lapsang?"

"Lapsang, please."

"A slice of cake, dear?"

"Yes, please, Aunt Flo. Thank you."

"Aunt Flo's cakes are better than ever, my dear."

"I'm sure. They always were delicious."

"Yes, there's something here that gives them that little extra bit of flavour. It must be the water."

"It's so lovely to see you again, David."

"Thank you, Aunt Edith. It's lovely to see you too. And looking so well, all of you."

"Oh yes, we're all very well. And very happy, aren't we, dears?"

"We certainly are," said Aunts Doris and Flo in unison.

"So how do you spend your time?" asked David, looking from one to another of his great-aunts' beaming rosy faces.

"Oh, this and that," said Aunt Flo. "I do a lot of cooking. And everything turns out so wonderfully."

"It certainly does, Flo dear," said Aunt Doris. "You're a marvellous cook. We're very lucky." She turned to David. "I must show you my embroidery after tea, dear. It seems to have taken me over."

"Doris does some really beautiful work, don't you, Doris. Such detail – I wouldn't have believed it possible."

"And what about your painting, Edith?" said Doris. "She had an exhibition, you know," she went on, turning to David. "Everyone came and they were all so complimentary."

"I seem to have a sort of guiding hand when I paint now. It's so very pleasing."

David grinned at his great-aunts' varied enthusiasms. Heaven certainly seems to be suiting them, he thought. He looked round the big sitting-room, just like the room they used to have, cluttered with furniture, pictures, books and general bric-a-brac. In one corner was a spinning-wheel with fragments of wool still on it. Leaning against a bookcase was an easel bearing a half-finished landscape. The walls were covered with pictures, tapestries and samplers, most of them the work of one or other of his aunts. Against one wall was an upright piano and he remembered that Aunt Edith had been no mean performer. She'd always said that music spoke to the soul in a way that no other art form did.

On a table was evidence of book-binding work

"Who's doing the book-binding?" he asked. "I don't remember that."

"Oh, that's Aunt Flo," said Doris. "She's only taken it up recently, haven't you, Flo dear?"

"Yes, I suddenly had this urge and it's been a wonderful pastime. I don't know why I never did it before."

They all looked so happy and contented and pleased with themselves that David just had to smile. The three of them had always lived together and none of them had ever married. Aunt Flo had had a near escape with a stockbroker who went on to marry three times in all, each time losing his older and richer wife to premature illness and death. His name had never been mentioned again.

Together they had looked after and ultimately nursed their mother after their father's early death. David had loved going to visit them because they were always so cheerful and uncomplaining in spite of having very little money and putting up with a series of painful and debilitating illnesses. He had always been warmly welcomed with hugs and home cooking and had never gone away empty-handed.

"And how's dear Ruth?" asked Aunt Doris gently. "Do you ever see her?"

"I have done, yes, but I don't now," replied David. "It doesn't seem to help her and I don't really feel the need to."

"So sad for those who are left behind," sighed Aunt Edith. "I remember when our dear mother died."

"Our faith brought us through, didn't

it," said Aunt Flo. "And that dear clergyman. What was his name?"

"Peter Ansell," said Aunt Edith promptly. She had always acted as their collective memory which meant that neither of the other two ever felt it necessary to remember anything.

"Such a dear man," put in Aunt Doris. "And he kept getting us muddled up, do you remember?" They all giggled delightedly. "And it's not as if we're alike at all," she added.

David grinned, recalling the difficulty he had had in telling them apart as a boy.

"I wonder what happened to him," mused Aunt Flo. "He moved on to another parish after that."

"And we got that lady vicar, do you remember?" put in Aunt Edith. "Not quite the same as dear Peter," she sighed, "but still a lovely person," she added brightly.

"It just doesn't matter, does it," said Aunt Doris. "All this silly nonsense about lady vicars. We felt like banging all their heads together, didn't we, dears."

"We did," replied Aunts Edith and Flo in unison.

"Well, I wish you had," said David. "It got the Church into a terrible muddle and still isn't resolved."

"So very silly," murmured Aunt Doris.

"And do you see my grandparents?" asked David.

"Dear Mary and Kenneth," said Aunt Flo. "Yes, we do. Of course you never knew them, did you. So sad. Oh, you must come again and we'll have them to tea. I'm sure they'd love to meet you."

"Yes, I'd like that very much," said David.

His maternal grandparents had always been a bit of a mystery. They had died during a trip to South America before David was born. Yellow fever was the generally accepted explanation but his parents had always talked about it as if there was some other less natural cause of death. Consequently David had always thought of them in rather romantic terms and was thrilled at the prospect of meeting them.

"And are you doing much sailing, dear?" asked Aunt Edith.

"Oh lots," exclaimed David, his face lighting up. "It's really wonderful here, with perfect conditions. I can't get enough of it."

"That's lovely, dear," said Aunt Flo, "but do be careful, won't you. Such a dangerous thing to do."

"Oh, don't worry about that," laughed David. "No harm will come to me here."

"Of course not, dear. How silly of me," said Aunt Flo, beaming at him so happily that David felt tears pricking his eyes and was overcome by a sudden rush of affection towards his aunts.

"It really is lovely to see you all again," he said, his voice breaking slightly. "You're wonderful and I love you all."

"Oh, that's lovely, dear," said Aunt Doris, "isn't it, dears."

"Indeed it is," said Aunts Edith and Flo in unison.

*

David stopped and leaned on the gate to admire the view. He was in a landscape of gently undulating hills, velvety green in the early morning sunshine. There was still dew on the grass and the air was soft and bracing. He loved early morning walks when he could be on his own and enjoy the peace and beauty of the countryside. He had always lived in the country and couldn't understand those who revelled in the noise and bustle of town or city. Andy had offered to take him to the 'Golden City' but he had declined. Beautiful and radiant it may be but he was much happier here, surrounded by open countryside and good fresh air.

Suddenly he felt that he was no longer alone and, looking round, he saw a man leaning on the gate beside him. But this was no ordinary man. Sprouting from his shoulder blades was a pair of enormous snow-white wings.

The angel turned to David and smiled.

"We meet at last," he said in a deep velvety voice. "I am Himmilech, your guardian angel. You've never seen me but I've always been there at your side since the moment you were conceived in your mother's womb. I watched over you, looked after you, tried to keep you from straying too far off the straight and narrow – not always easy! – and picked you up when you fell. Now you're here and safe for ever. My job is done and I've come to say farewell."

David smiled, entranced by the beautiful creature before him. He'd always believed in guardian angels and often felt he'd benefited from someone being there to help. And now here he was, standing in front of him.

"Thank you," he said at last. "Thank you for all you did for me. I did half suspect you were there sometimes and it's wonderful to meet you at last."

"Well, you gave me a few anxious

moments and it's a good thing I'm a strong swimmer!" mused Himmilech. "But that was the easy part. The hard bit is keeping the devil at bay. But you did well and my job was relatively easy."

"And at the end?"

"What will be will be," said Himmilech. "There are some things I can't do anything about. Rejoice that you are here. Now you know that earthly life is but an introduction to where you're really meant to be."

David turned away and looked over the green landscape, felt the growing warmth of the sun on his back, heard the song of the birds and felt again the golden light glow within him.

"Yes, it's beautiful here," he sighed, "more beautiful than anything I could ever have imagined."

"God is with you, my friend," said Himmilech softly, raising his hand in blessing.

David turned to look at him but found himself alone. He felt the glow spread within him. Lifting his face to the sky, he closed his eyes and whispered, "Thank you, Lord" as the light overcame him entirely and the song of angels filled his heart. "Praise to the Holiest in the height," they sang, "and in the depth be praise."

✻

"Michael!"

David had spotted him across the road and was running to catch him up.

"Michael! Stop!" he panted as he caught up with the other man and put his hand on his shoulder. He turned.

"David! Wonderful to see you!"

"And you. I knew it was you. You haven't changed at all."

"Nor you," said Michael with a broad grin.

"Well, we did share a room for a year."

"Yes, a very small room! You get to know someone pretty well in those circumstances."

"Especially when they play all the Brahms symphonies one after the other over and over again at full volume. It's a wonder I ever passed any exams!"

"But you like his music?"

"I do actually – he's one of my favourites. I can't think why!"

"Well, I've moved on since then. It's now Mahler – and I really don't think I'll ever go off him." A sudden thought struck him. "Are you doing anything at the moment?"

"No," said David, "I don't think so."

"Come with me then. He's conducting a new work. I'm on my way there now. I never miss anything he does."

"Mahler himself?"

"The very same. It's called 'Song of the Heavens'. It'll blow your soul!"

*

"It's all about love, you see."

"Paul Croucher said it was all about death."

She smiled.

"Yes, I've heard him too. And very persuasive he is! And he's right. Death was our big hang-up. It overshadowed everything, determined our whole attitude and behaviour. You can't understand anything unless you put death in its place. And it's love that diminishes death, puts it in perspective, looses its hold on people's hearts and minds. In the face of love death is nothing. Preoccupation with death is preoccupation with self and preoccupation with self precludes love. You cannot love if everything you do is centred on yourself."

"What about 'Love your neighbour as yourself'?" asked David. "It's always puzzled me. Very few people actually loved themselves and those that did didn't seem capable of loving anyone else!"

"Yes, exactly! But it's such a wonderful saying. Because what it's actually doing is defining the nature of love. We know we're supposed to love our neighbour because Jesus told us – many times. And we know in what way we're not supposed to love ourselves – selfishly - he told us that too. What this saying tells us is that love for ourselves and love for our neighbour are one and the same thing. Love – proper love – is what meets both sets of criteria. It shouldn't be indulgent and exclusive and selfish and all take-and-no-give. It should be caring and forgiving and gentle and accepting. Then you can see that it's the same love we should feel for ourselves as for others. And when we feel and act on that love, then we're doing God's will. And that's how it is here in heaven. God's will is done." She paused and looked wistful. "It could be done on earth too. It really could. Christians pray for it every day in the words of the Lord's Prayer but do they really understand what they're praying for and what it requires them to do?"

There was silence. Her eyes gazed into the distance and an expression of deep sadness came over her face. David felt compelled to lean forward and touch her hand in comfort. She grasped both his hands in hers and looked at him with overflowing eyes.

"There is so much pain and suffering. So much. And all for want of love."

Suddenly she brightened.

"But we've got to have faith," she exclaimed vehemently. "The battle isn't yet done."

Her eyes flashed and David half expected her to stand up and paw the ground like a bull about to charge.

"Steady on, Annie," he laughed. "It's only me!"

She laughed too.

"Yes, I do get rather carried away, don't I," she said. "It's just so important. If only I could have done more."

David had never met her or heard of her. The only clue to her earthly identity was a slight South African accent.

"Forgive me," he said, "but who were you and what did you do?"

"It's no wonder you don't know me. You were too young and anyway very little of what we did leaked into the outside world. I was one of a group who tried to help the black people during the period of apartheid in South Africa." She broke off. "You've been there, haven't you?"

"Yes, I loved it."

She nodded as if any other answer was impossible then resumed.

"We weren't politicians or priests or lawyers, just ordinary folk sickened by the way people were being treated by the regime. The extent of what was going on wasn't even known by the majority of white people in South Africa. We tried to broadcast it but not very successfully. We did what we could in terms of providing money and refuge for people who needed it but the effects were limited. The regime was just too strong.." Her face lit up. "We sheltered Nelson Mandela once when he was on the run. Such a lovely man. So strong and yet so gentle." She paused. "You know," she went on, "what happened there when apartheid was dismantled was genuinely a miracle. The work of Mandela and Desmond Tutu and others who conceived the idea of the Truth and Reconciliation Commission and made it work in spite of all the opposition was an example of love and forgiveness in its most wonderful form. So much pain and suffering had been inflicted and yet it was forgiven, not just by one or two individuals but by a whole people. And now?"

She was silent for a moment.

"May God continue to bless that beautiful land," she sighed.

*

"**Y**ou don't remember me, do you?"

"I'm sorry, I'm afraid I don't."

"You gave me a fiver when I was down and out. I never forgot. It saved my life. I was all ready to give up then you came along. I'd lost all hope and would have jumped in the river or something stupid. But that fiver changed everything. I went and had a slap-up meal – well, it was for me – slept like a log and the next morning went along to one of those shelter places and it all happened from there. I ended up doing a computer course, got a decent job, met someone, had a couple of kids. I managed to help a few other people in the same situation as I'd been in. Then I got ill – effects of all that bad living, I suppose – and here I am. But I just wanted to thank you. None of it would have happened without that fiver. God bless you, my friend."

David was motoring back to his mooring after a wonderful day's sailing. The sun was low on the horizon but the air was still balmy and warm. During the day a fresh breeze had provided perfect sailing conditions and now the wind had dropped to give calm water and a lazy evening stillness.

Looking to his right where the shore flattened to a gently sloping sandy beach, David saw a man waving to him. There was a thin trail of smoke rising beside him and David guessed he had lit a small barbecue for a picnic supper. The man continued waving and David decided to go closer in to have a look. It might be the man was in trouble although there didn't seem to be anything panicky in his gestures.

He turned the boat and approached the beach. As he got nearer he switched off the engine and glided the boat in until it grounded gently on the soft sand. Leaping off, he turned towards the man who was now stooping over his barbecue. He saw David and straightened up.

"Welcome," he called. "Come and join me."

David started to walk towards him. When he got close enough to look into the man's eyes, he felt an irresistible attraction that made him begin to run, stumbling slightly in the sand but feeling an inexplicable excitement rising within him. As he got nearer, the man held out his arms but David staggered and sank to his knees in front of him.

"Come, David," said the man gently.

David took his hands and pulled himself to his feet. He couldn't take his eyes off the other's face and the look of tenderness and concern on his features. His eyes were deep-set and magnetic. David could only gaze into them, feeling his whole being absorbed into their depths. As he gazed, a golden light emanated from the man's head and body and streamed out towards him. He sank to his knees again.

"Lord Jesus," he whispered.

"Get up, my child, and come to me," said Jesus.

He helped David to his feet and embraced him. David half-fell against him. He put his arms round him and leaned his head on his shoulder, relaxing into the warmth of his body. The light surrounded and filled him and he felt a growing lightness as if he was floating off the ground. The light and the lightness grew, every sense overflowing with colour and music. A sudden dazzling brightness overcame him and he heard that gentle beloved voice in his ear.

"Rest, my child, rest. For I am with you to the end of time."

✢

The decision had been taken. A small group stood around the bed and watched as a doctor switched off the life-support system. For the first time there was complete silence in the small hospital room.

They looked down at the still figure in the bed, his features relaxed into what seemed like a half-smile.

"He's at peace now," someone said.

*

The white and gold light bathed him in its translucence and music of breathtaking beauty swirled around him. Some of it was familiar but much of it was new – strange and mysterious, flowing inexorably on through magic harmonies and rhythms, great climaxes and periods of almost complete stillness. The music and the light pierced into his very depths and he felt his heart bursting with a joy the like of which he had never experienced. It was not a passing joy of thrill or excitement but a deep and absorbing happiness which filled his whole being until he himself was an integral part of the light and the sound and the swirling throng.

This, he knew, was where he belonged, what he was made for and where he would now forever be....